A hush fell over the crowd as Hen Haus revealed the new school crest: *Always Kind*.

Mable and all her friends cheered loudly.

Mable's mom smiled and said proudly, "That's my Beautiful Mable."

On graduation day, the Head Hen awarded Mable the school's highest honor.

"This year's Hen of the Haus award goes to Mable, whose kindness has made this a better place for all of us."

The chicks applauded for their friend.

"And because of Mable and her example," the Head Hen continued, "I've decided it's time to change our school's motto!"

The Head Hen
loved seeing
all her chicks
so happy. She
was thankful to
have Mable as a
student. *Mable's
kindness is
contagious!*
she thought.

Pretty soon, Mable and Otilia's kindness began to spread. As springtime bloomed at Hen Haus, the chicks began to value kindness more than plumpness, prettiness, or productivity.

"That's all so hard to keep up with," confessed Vivian.

"Kindness feels so much better and makes me feel so much happier!" said Beatrice.

"You're funny, Elliotte."

"Can I help you with that, Gertrude?"

Like Mable, Otilia then went out of her way to be kind to all the other chicks.

"You look so pretty, Mia!"

But Mable's friendship was more important to Otilia than what other chicks thought about her. And it was more important than being plump or pretty or productive.

Otilia, now a 2-P, was very thankful for Mable's kindness, and from that moment on, they were friends.

"Why is a 2-P friends with a No-P?" some chicks whispered.

"Really?" Otilia asked, surprised.

"Of course! You need it much more than I do!" Mable said, and gave her backpack to Otilia.

On a cold January morning, Mable arrived at class early to find Otilia crying.

"What's wrong, Otilia?" Mable asked.

"I lost my backpack." Otilia said sadly, "I don't know where to carry my egg."

Mable noticed the egg sitting on Otilia's desk. "Otilia, you laid an egg! I'm so excited for you!" Mable said immediately, "You can use my backpack!"

"Your kindness is a gift, Mable. It's a gift God gave you to help others. And it makes you so much more than plump or pretty or productive. It makes you beautiful."

Hearing that she was helping other chicks made Mable feel happy.

The Head Hen smiled. "Keep using your gift, Beautiful Mable."

"Mable, your being here is no mistake! I arranged for it myself."

"Really?" Mable asked, surprised.

The Head Hen explained, "I had heard of your kindness and thought that was something we could use more of here. And, you know what? I was right! You may not see it yet, but I can see the effect you are having on the other chicks."

One day, just before Christmas break,
Mable was called into the Head Hen's office.

"Mable, do you know why you are here?"
The Head Hen asked.

"I'm not sure." Mable answered, "Did I do
something wrong?"

"No." The Head Hen smiled, "Not why you
are here in my office, but why you are here
at Hen Haus?"

"Actually, that's something I wonder about
all the time." Mable confessed, "Maybe
there was some kind of a mistake?"

As the fall went on, Mable began to feel very, very bad about herself.

Why can't I be a 3-P? she wondered, *Why am I even at Hen Haus?*
She felt out of place and lonely.

Still, Mable went out of her way to be kind to all her classmates,
and her mom continued calling her Beautiful Mable.

"How was school, Beautiful Mable?" Mable's mom asked again as she arrived back at the coop. She was excited to hear about her daughter's second day.

"Please just call me Mable." Mable requested.

The next morning, Mable arrived early to class where she discovered another chick seated alone.

"Good morning, Otilia." Mable said, remembering her name from the day before.

Otilia was a 1-P (only plump). Her first day was almost as rough as Mable's.

"I love your backpack." Mable complimented Otilia.

Mable's kind words and smile made Otilia feel better. She was getting ready to thank Mable when Gertrude, Vivian, and Beatrice entered the room.

What would they think of me talking to a No-P? Otilia thought and said nothing.

Mable felt awful.
"No one wants to be my friend."

"How was school, Beautiful Mable?" Mable's mom asked as she arrived back at the coop, excited to hear about her daughter's first day.

"May I just go to my room?" Mable asked, not feeling like talking.

The fact is, most pullets at Hen Haus were already plump, pretty, and productive. Those chicks were known as 3-Ps. A few pullets were 2-Ps, and pitiful 1-Ps were extremely rare.

But Hen Haus had never ever, ever seen a No-P. That is, until Mable came along.

Mable felt awful. "I'm not plump, not pretty, and not productive."

The classroom erupted in laughter.

"Beautiful?" Gertrude snickered quietly. "Hardly. Homely, not pretty!"

"Scrawny, not plump!" Vivian said under her breath.

"Definitely not productive." whispered Beatrice.

"Cock-a-doodle-doo!"
crowed Beauregard,
the rooster from
across the pond,
officially beginning
the school day.

In homeroom,
the teacher took
attendance.

"Gertrude?" The
teacher called.
"Here!" Gertrude
responded.
"Vivian?"
"Here." Vivian
raised her wing.
"Beatrice?"
"Present!" Beatrice
said.
"Beautiful Mable?"
"I'm here!" Mable
chirped excitedly.

Mable was nervous as she entered the front gates of the campus. *Plump, Pretty, Productive* read the school crest.

Mable was eager to make friends with all the new chicks.

"You are so plump!" Mable smiled kindly as she complimented a chick passing by.
"Hmph." The plump chick responded, all but ignoring Mable.

Just then, another chick walked by with long eyelashes and a beautiful beak.
"You are very pretty!" Mable said.
The pretty chick turned her beak up and kept walking.

Another pullet strolled by with a backpack full of eggs! Mable was impressed with her productivity.
"Wow! You are..." Mable stopped as the productive chick kept going without noticing her.

Mable wasn't what you would call a fancy chicken, which is why she was very surprised to receive an invitation to attend Hen Haus, a very fancy school.

Only the finest chicks from the finest chicken families in the area attended Hen Haus. Mable's mother was very excited for her daughter. She dressed Mable up in her school uniform and fixed her feathers before sending her off to her first day.

"I'm so proud of you, Beautiful Mable!"

Mable was a *pullet*, a young female chicken. In one year, she would be a hen.

Mable's mom called her *Beautiful Mable* because Mable was kind and made everyone in her family feel special.

"You look so pretty, Mom!"
"You're funny, Ricky!"
"Can I help you with that, Dad?"

"Thank you, Beautiful Mable."

Beautiful Mable

© 2019 by Idealist-Gotzon Publishing

Written by Mike Nawrocki
Illustrated by Sara Jo Floyd
Art direction by Jenn Gotzon Chandler

978-1-7334694-1-8

Design by Chris Garborg | garborgdesign.com
Editorial services by Michelle Winger | literallyprecise.com

Printed in the United States of America.

19 20 21 22 23 24 25   7 6 5 4 3 2 1

Beautiful Mable

From the co-creator of VeggieTales

Mike Nawrocki

Illustrated by Sara Jo Floyd